W9-BFJ-578

Sylvie

To Paul, who always said this would happen.
And to Anna, who made it so.

Copyright © 2009 by Jennifer Sattler

All rights reserved.
Published in the United States by Dragonfly Books, an imprint of
Random House Children's Books, a division of Random House, Inc., New York.
Originally published in hardcover in the United States by Random House
Children's Books, New York, in 2009.

Dragonfly Books with the colophon is a registered trademark of Random House, Inc.

Visit us on the Web! randomhouse.com/kids

Educators and librarians, for a variety of teaching tools,
visit us at RHTeachersLibrarians.com

The Library of Congress has cataloged the hardcover edition of this work as follows:
Sattler, Jennifer Gordon.
Sylvie / by Jennifer Sattler. —1st ed.
p. cm.
Summary: When Sylvie the pink flamingo learns her color comes from the little pink shrimp she eats,
she decides to expand her choices, trying everything under the sun and, unfortunately, overdoing it.
ISBN 978-0-375-85708-9 (trade) — ISBN 978-0-375-95708-6 (lib. bdg.)
[1. Flamingos—Fiction. 2. Birds—Fiction. 3. Food—Fiction.] I. Title.
PZ7.S24935Sy 2009 [E]—dc22 2008011259

ISBN 978-0-449-81072-9 (pbk.)

MANUFACTURED IN CHINA
10 9 8 7 6 5 4 3 2 1
First Dragonfly Books Edition

Sylvie

Written and illustrated by
Jennifer Sattler

DRAGONFLY BOOKS · NEW YORK

One morning, Sylvie looked at her family.

Then she looked around at everything else.

"Mama," she asked, "why are we pink?"

"Well, dear, we're pink because the little shrimp we eat are pink," said Mama.

"Hmmm . . ."
That gave Sylvie an idea.

She tried nibbling on some palm leaves.

Sure enough, she started to turn green!

Next she spotted some
delicious-looking grapes.

The grapes turned Sylvie positively purple!

But Sylvie didn't stop there!
She thought she'd look *yummy* in chocolate!

She was right!

"What a beautiful sky!" said Sylvie.
"It's the perfect shade of . . ."

". . . blue!"

Sylvie just happened to be flying by a kite . . .

. . . and became Scarlet Sylvie
with just one bite!

What fun she was having!
She wondered what stripes might taste like.

"Hmmm . . . rather stripy."

Why wear flowers on just your head . . .

. . . when you can be a whole bouquet!

Sylvie had to tiptoe across the sand
for a taste of swimsuit.

It was worth it, to be paisley!

But after stuffing her tummy all day,
Sylvie didn't feel so well.

In fact, Sylvie didn't feel like Sylvie at all.

She looked at herself.
Then she looked at her family.

Sylvie decided to go back
to eating little pink shrimp . . .

. . . with a little dessert.